MARVEL® SUPER HERO SQUAD

HULKED·OUT SQUADDIES!

WRITER: Todd Dezago
ARTISTS: Leonel Castellani & Marcelo DiChiara
COLORS: Sotocolor
LETTERS: Dave Sharpe

SUPER HERO SQUAD STRIPS
WRITER: Paul Tobin
ARTISTS: Marcelo DiChiara, Todd Nauck & Dario Brizuela
COLORS: Chris Sotomayor
LETTERS: Blambot's Nate Piekos

ASSISTANT EDITOR: Michael Horwitz
EDITOR: Nathan Cosby

Visit us at www.abdopublishing.com

Reinforced library bound edition published in 2011 by Spotlight, a division of the ABDO Group, 8000 West 78th Street, Edina, Minnesota 55439. Spotlight produces high-quality reinforced library bound editions for schools and libraries. Published by agreement with Marvel Characters, Inc.

Printed in the United States of America, North Mankato, Minnesota.
102010
012011
♺ This book contains at least 10% recycled materials.

Library of Congress Cataloging-in-Publication Data

Dezago, Todd.
  Hulked-out squaddies! / Todd Dezago, writer ; Leonel Castellani, artist ; Sotocolor, colors ; Dave Sharpe, letters. -- Reinforced library bound ed.
      p. cm. -- (Super hero squad)
  "Marvel."
  ISBN 978-1-59961-859-3
  1. Graphic novels. [1. Graphic novels. 2. Superheroes--Fiction.] I. Castellani, Leonel, ill. II. Title.
  PZ7.7.D508Hu 2011
  741.5'973--dc22
                                        2010027323

All Spotlight books have reinforced library bindings and
are manufactured in the United States of America.

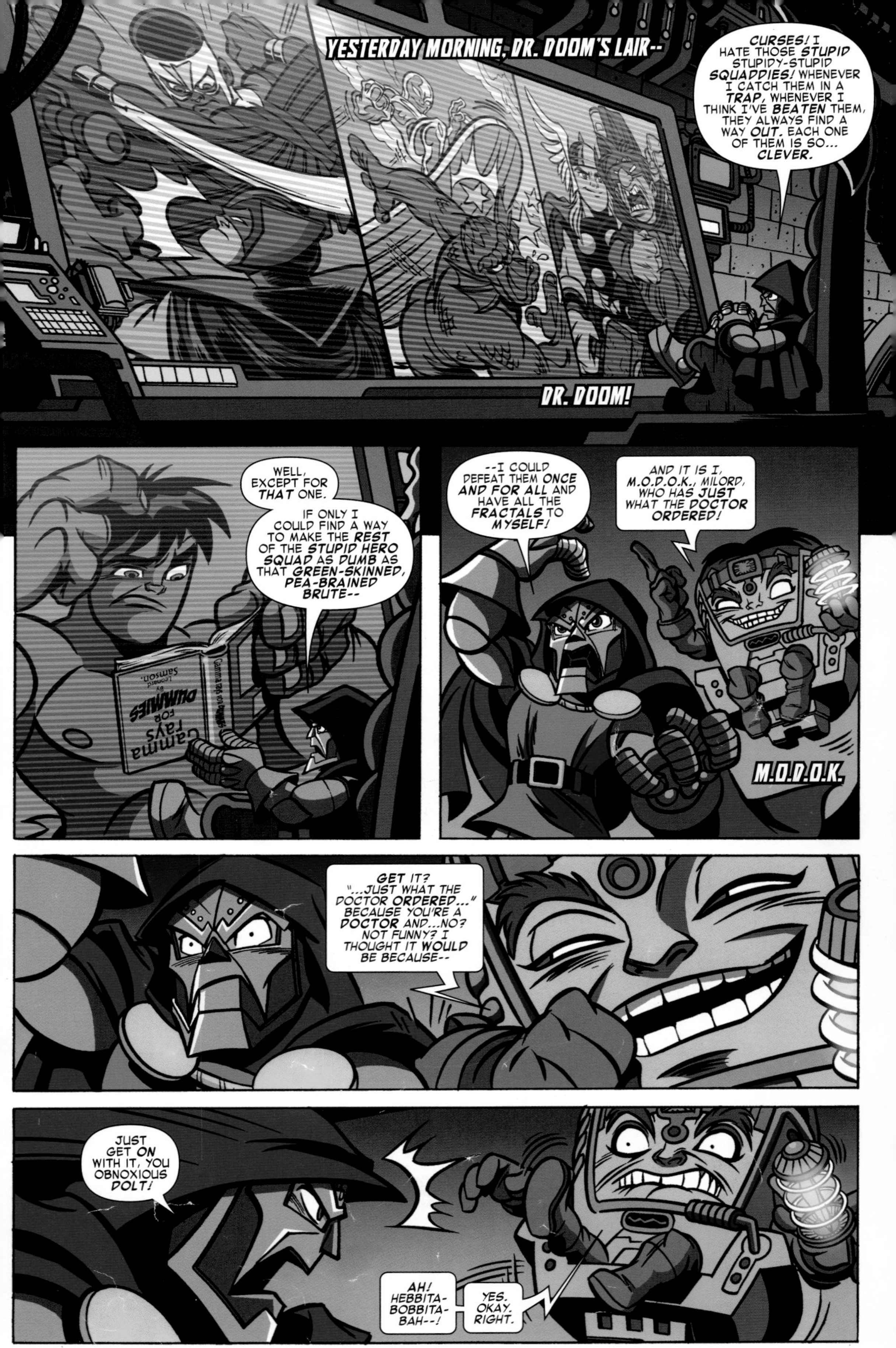
YESTERDAY MORNING, DR. DOOM'S LAIR--
CURSES! I HATE THOSE STUPID STUPIDY-STUPID SQUADDIES! WHENEVER I CATCH THEM IN A TRAP, WHENEVER I THINK I'VE BEATEN THEM, THEY ALWAYS FIND A WAY OUT. EACH ONE OF THEM IS SO... CLEVER.
DR. DOOM!
WELL, EXCEPT FOR THAT ONE.
IF ONLY I COULD FIND A WAY TO MAKE THE REST OF THE STUPID HERO SQUAD AS DUMB AS THAT GREEN-SKINNED, PEA-BRAINED BRUTE--
Gamma rays FOR DUMMIES by Leonard Samson.
--I COULD DEFEAT THEM ONCE AND FOR ALL AND HAVE ALL THE FRACTALS TO MYSELF!
AND IT IS I, M.O.D.O.K., MILORD, WHO HAS JUST WHAT THE DOCTOR ORDERED!
M.O.D.O.K.
GET IT? "...JUST WHAT THE DOCTOR ORDERED..." BECAUSE YOU'RE A DOCTOR AND...NO? NOT FUNNY? I THOUGHT IT WOULD BE BECAUSE--
JUST GET ON WITH IT, YOU OBNOXIOUS DOLT!
AH! HEBBITA-BOBBITA-BAH--!
YES. OKAY. RIGHT.

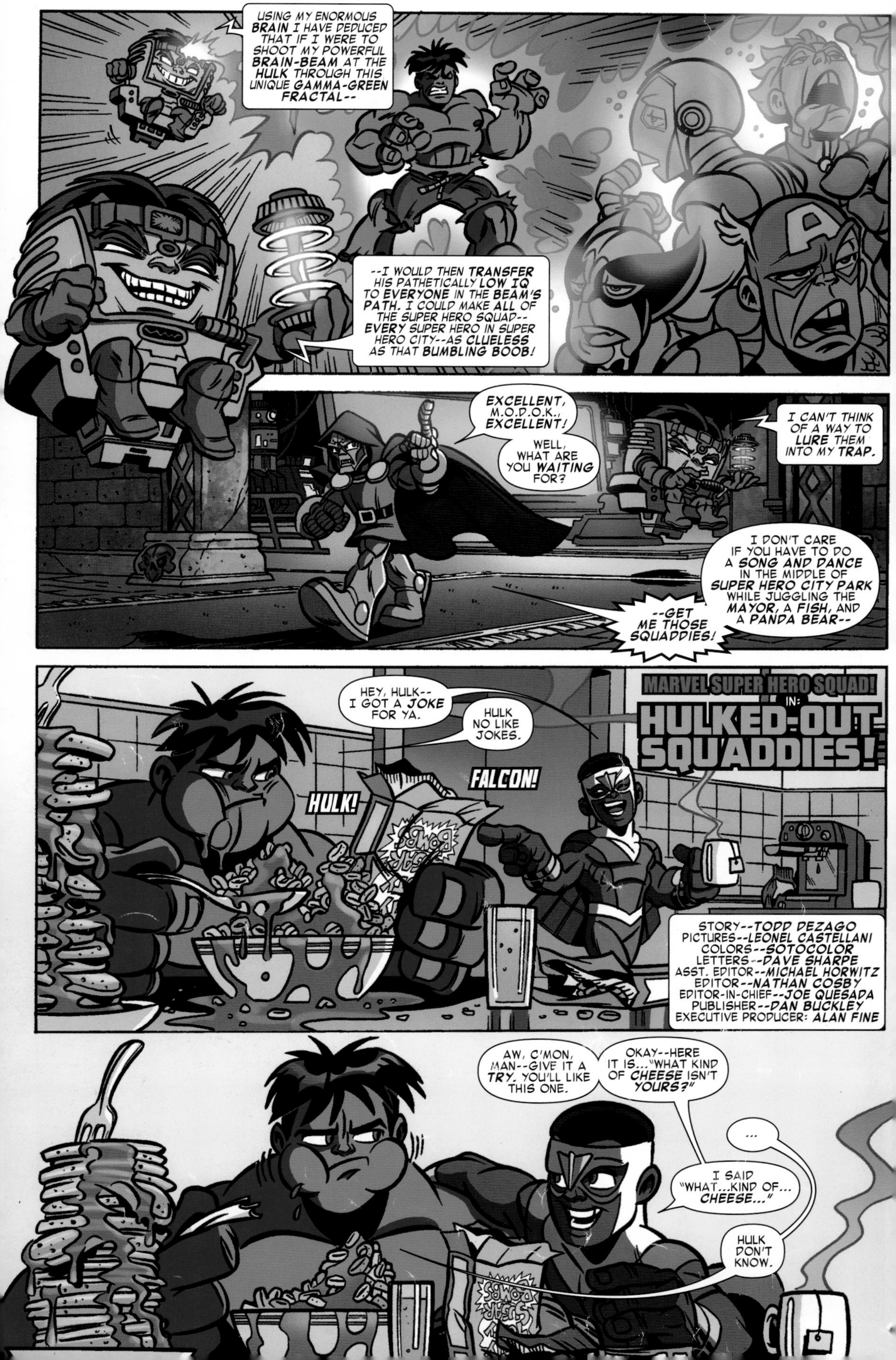
USING MY ENORMOUS BRAIN I HAVE DEDUCED THAT IF I WERE TO SHOOT MY POWERFUL BRAIN-BEAM AT THE HULK THROUGH THIS UNIQUE GAMMA-GREEN FRACTAL--
--I WOULD THEN TRANSFER HIS PATHETICALLY LOW IQ TO EVERYONE IN THE BEAM'S PATH. I COULD MAKE ALL OF THE SUPER HERO SQUAD-- EVERY SUPER HERO IN SUPER HERO CITY--AS CLUELESS AS THAT BUMBLING BOOB!
EXCELLENT, M.O.D.O.K., EXCELLENT!
WELL, WHAT ARE YOU WAITING FOR?
I CAN'T THINK OF A WAY TO LURE THEM INTO MY TRAP.
I DON'T CARE IF YOU HAVE TO DO A SONG AND DANCE IN THE MIDDLE OF SUPER HERO CITY PARK WHILE JUGGLING THE MAYOR, A FISH, AND A PANDA BEAR--
--GET ME THOSE SQUADDIES!
MARVEL SUPER HERO SQUAD! IN:
HULKED-OUT SQUADDIES!
HEY, HULK-- I GOT A JOKE FOR YA.
HULK NO LIKE JOKES.
HULK!
FALCON!
STORY--TODD DEZAGO
PICTURES--LEONEL CASTELLANI
COLORS--SOTOCOLOR
LETTERS--DAVE SHARPE
ASST. EDITOR--MICHAEL HORWITZ
EDITOR--NATHAN COSBY
EDITOR-IN-CHIEF--JOE QUESADA
PUBLISHER--DAN BUCKLEY
EXECUTIVE PRODUCER: ALAN FINE
AW, C'MON, MAN--GIVE IT A TRY. YOU'LL LIKE THIS ONE.
OKAY--HERE IT IS... "WHAT KIND OF CHEESE ISN'T YOURS?"
...
I SAID "WHAT...KIND OF... CHEESE..."
HULK DON'T KNOW.

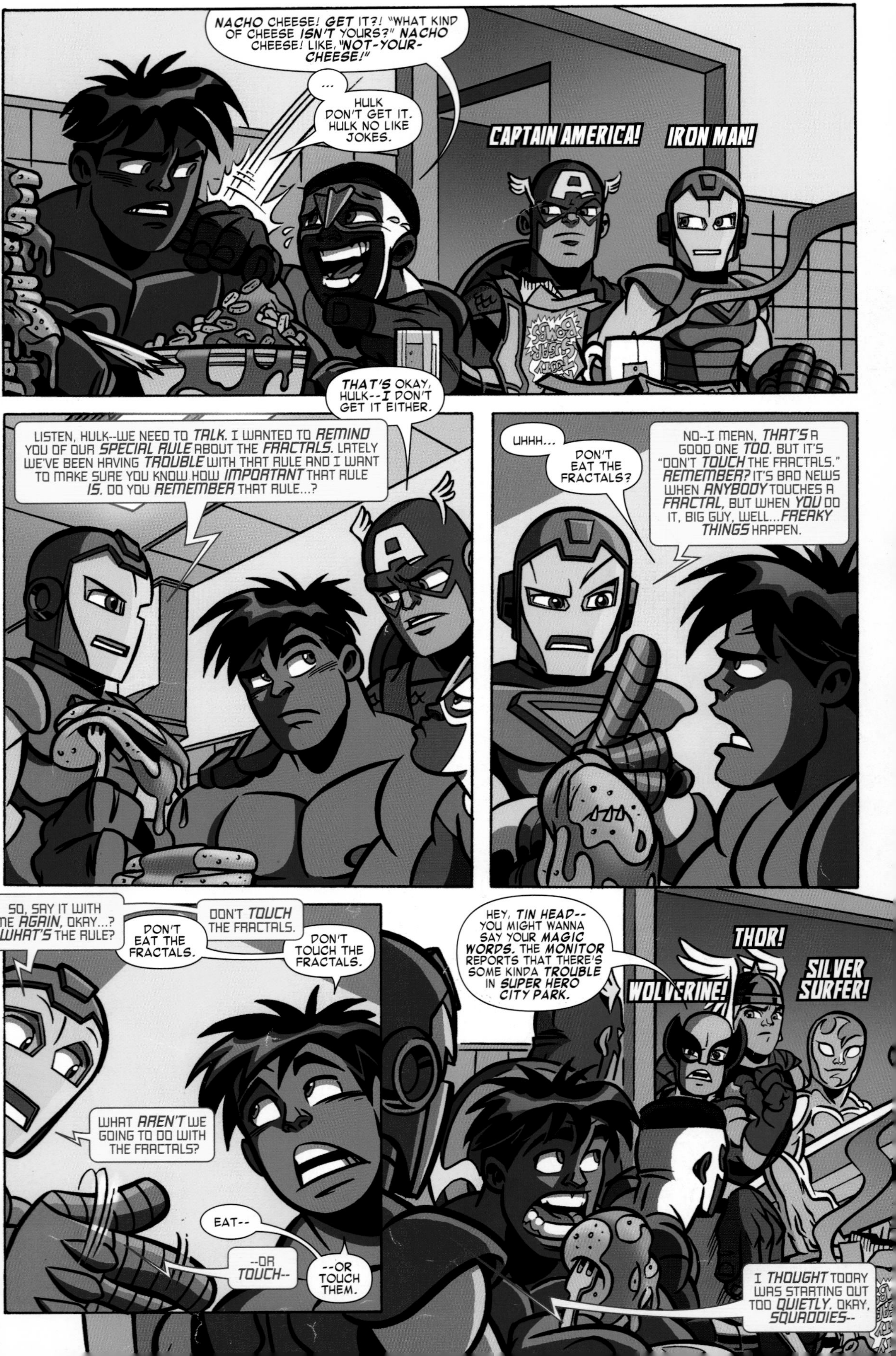

NACHO CHEESE! GET IT?! "WHAT KIND OF CHEESE ISN'T YOURS?" NACHO CHEESE! LIKE, "NOT-YOUR-CHEESE!"
...
HULK DON'T GET IT. HULK NO LIKE JOKES.
CAPTAIN AMERICA!
IRON MAN!
THAT'S OKAY, HULK--I DON'T GET IT EITHER.
LISTEN, HULK--WE NEED TO TALK. I WANTED TO REMIND YOU OF OUR SPECIAL RULE ABOUT THE FRACTALS. LATELY WE'VE BEEN HAVING TROUBLE WITH THAT RULE AND I WANT TO MAKE SURE YOU KNOW HOW IMPORTANT THAT RULE IS. DO YOU REMEMBER THAT RULE...?
UHHH...
DON'T EAT THE FRACTALS?
NO--I MEAN, THAT'S A GOOD ONE TOO. BUT IT'S "DON'T TOUCH THE FRACTALS." REMEMBER? IT'S BAD NEWS WHEN ANYBODY TOUCHES A FRACTAL, BUT WHEN YOU DO IT, BIG GUY, WELL...FREAKY THINGS HAPPEN.
SO, SAY IT WITH ME AGAIN, OKAY...? WHAT'S THE RULE?
DON'T EAT THE FRACTALS.
DON'T TOUCH THE FRACTALS.
DON'T TOUCH THE FRACTALS.
WHAT AREN'T WE GOING TO DO WITH THE FRACTALS?
EAT--
--OR TOUCH--
--OR TOUCH THEM.
HEY, TIN HEAD--YOU MIGHT WANNA SAY YOUR MAGIC WORDS. THE MONITOR REPORTS THAT THERE'S SOME KINDA TROUBLE IN SUPER HERO CITY PARK.
WOLVERINE!
THOR!
SILVER SURFER!
I THOUGHT TODAY WAS STARTING OUT TOO QUIETLY. OKAY, SQUADDIES--

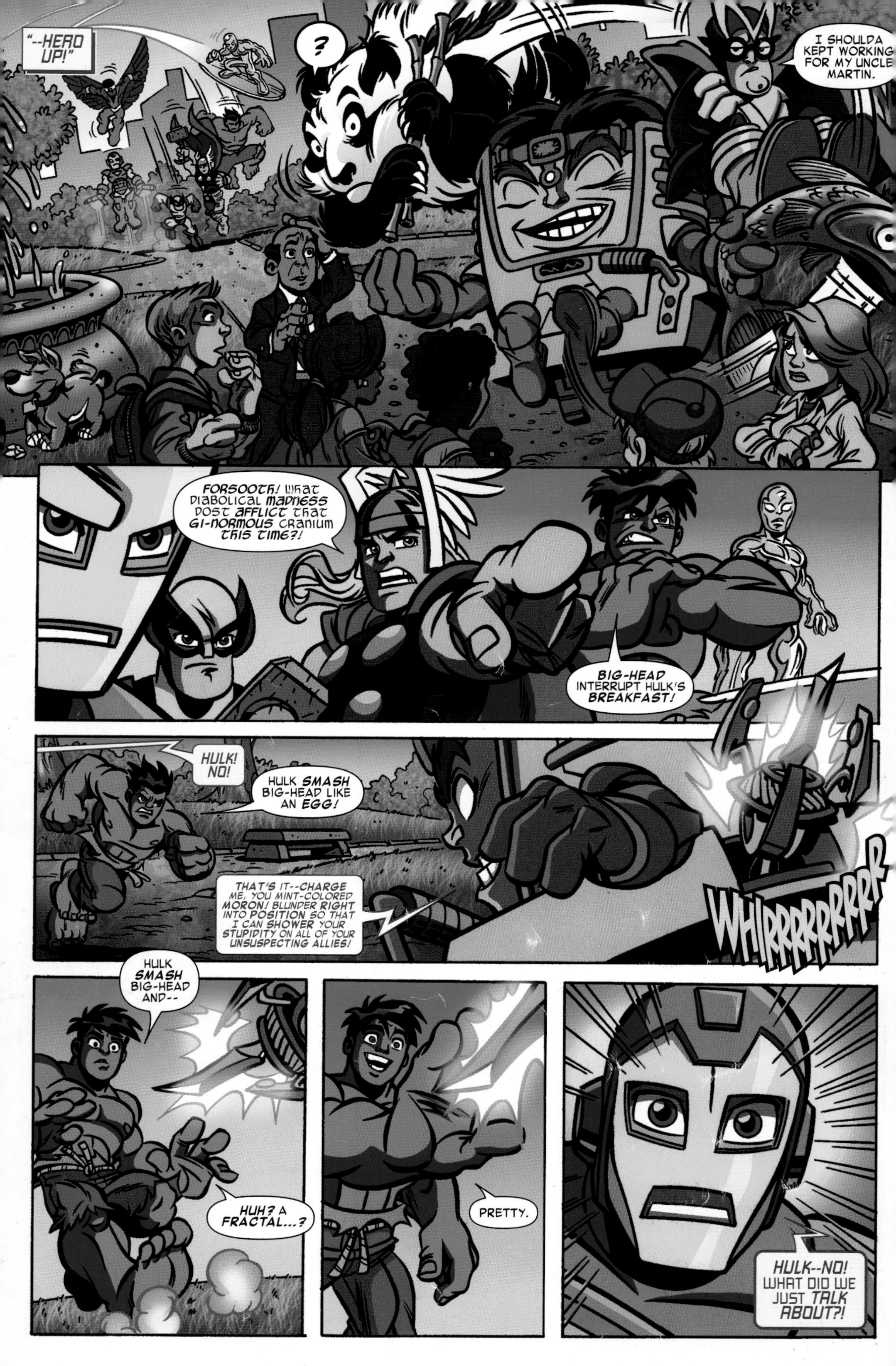
"--HERO UP!"
?
I SHOULDA KEPT WORKING FOR MY UNCLE MARTIN.
FORSOOTH! WHAT DIABOLICAL MADNESS DOST AFFLICT THAT GI-NORMOUS CRANIUM THIS TIME?!
BIG-HEAD INTERRUPT HULK'S BREAKFAST!
HULK! NO!
HULK SMASH BIG-HEAD LIKE AN EGG!
THAT'S IT--CHARGE ME, YOU MINT-COLORED MORON! BLUNDER RIGHT INTO POSITION SO THAT I CAN SHOWER YOUR STUPIDITY ON ALL OF YOUR UNSUSPECTING ALLIES!
WHIRRRRRRRR
HULK SMASH BIG-HEAD AND--
HUH? A FRACTAL...?
PRETTY.
HULK--NO! WHAT DID WE JUST TALK ABOUT?!

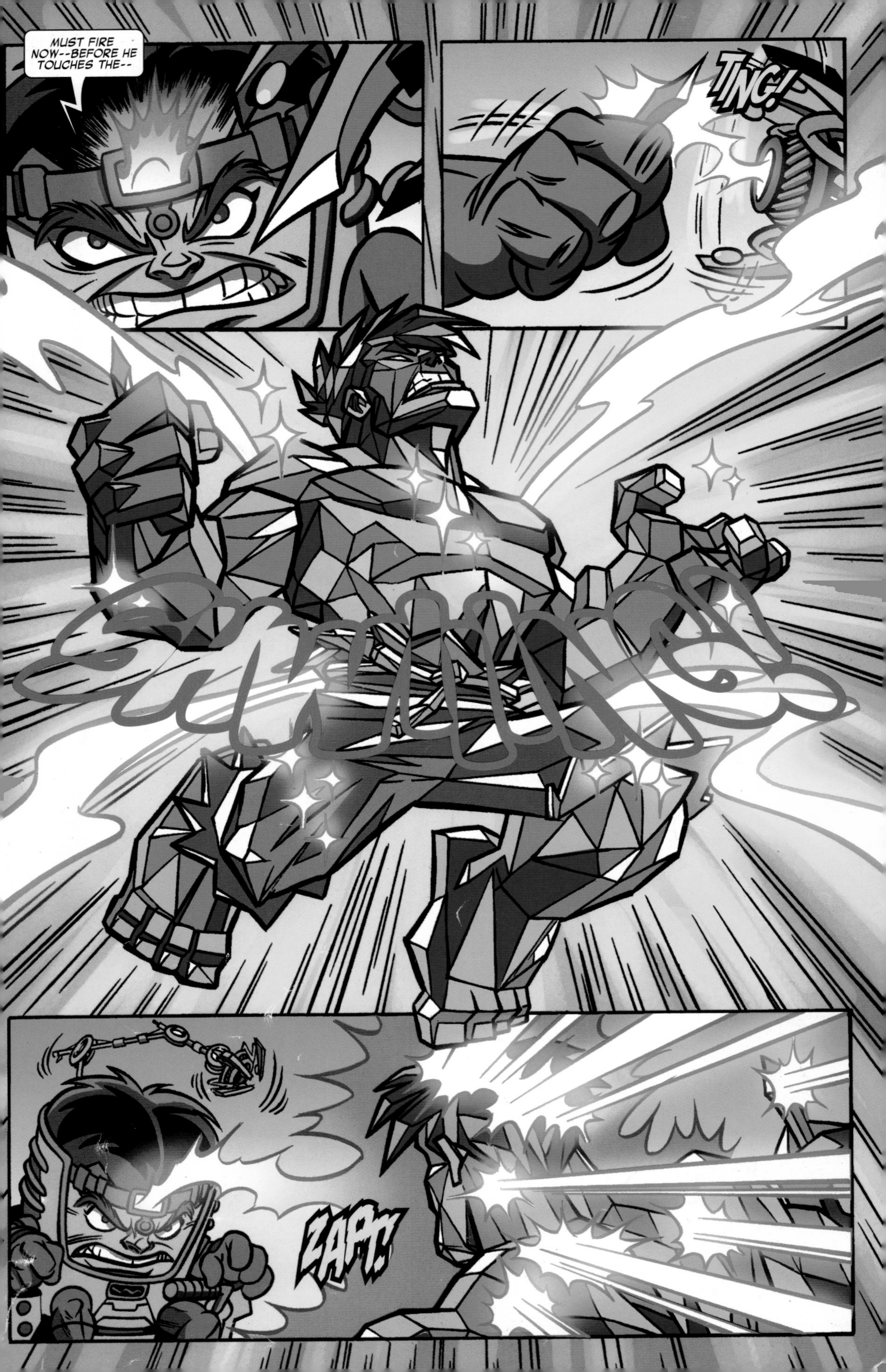
MUST FIRE NOW--BEFORE HE TOUCHES THE--
TNG!
ZAP!

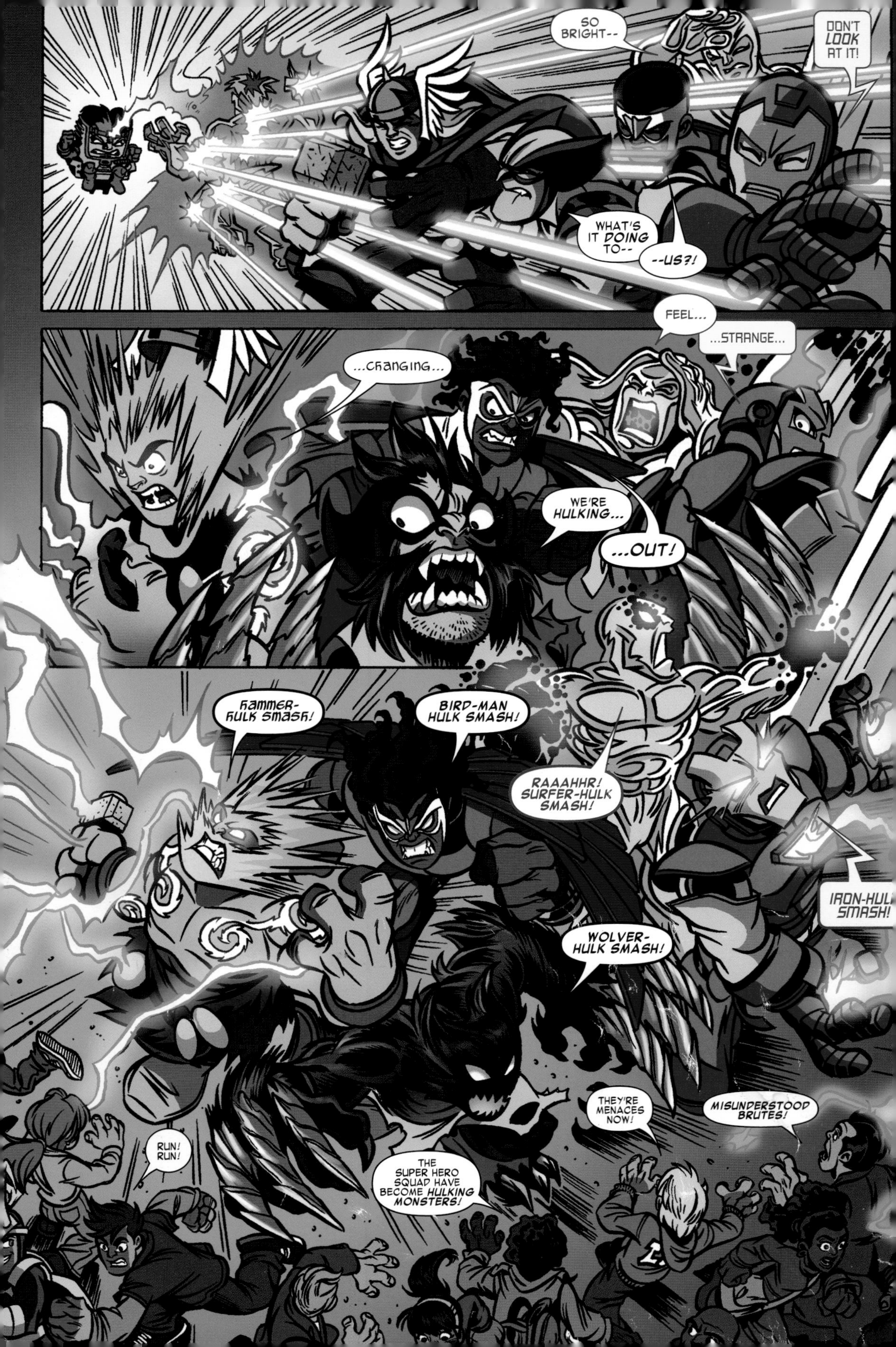
SO BRIGHT--
DON'T LOOK AT IT!
WHAT'S IT DOING TO--
--US?!
FEEL...
...STRANGE...
...CHANGING...
WE'RE HULKING...
...OUT!
HAMMER-HULK SMASH!
BIRD-MAN HULK SMASH!
RAAAHHR! SURFER-HULK SMASH!
IRON-HULK SMASH!
WOLVER-HULK SMASH!
RUN! RUN!
THEY'RE MENACES NOW!
MISUNDERSTOOD BRUTES!
THE SUPER HERO SQUAD HAVE BECOME HULKING MONSTERS!

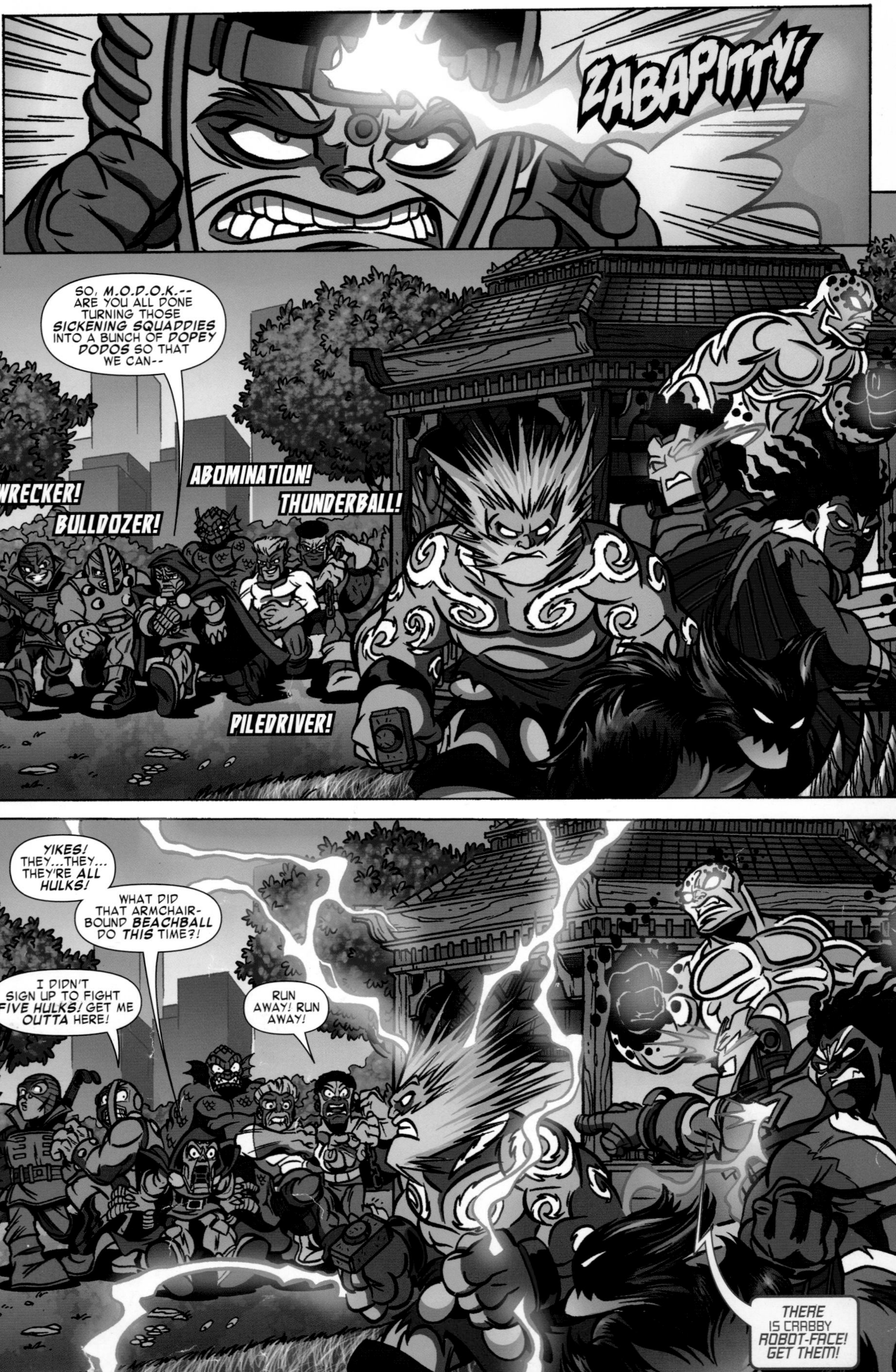
ZABAPITTY!
SO, M.O.D.O.K.--ARE YOU ALL DONE TURNING THOSE SICKENING SQUADDIES INTO A BUNCH OF DOPEY DODOS SO THAT WE CAN--
WRECKER!
BULLDOZER!
ABOMINATION!
THUNDERBALL!
PILEDRIVER!
YIKES! THEY...THEY... THEY'RE ALL HULKS!
WHAT DID THAT ARMCHAIR-BOUND BEACHBALL DO THIS TIME?!
I DIDN'T SIGN UP TO FIGHT FIVE HULKS! GET ME OUTTA HERE!
RUN AWAY! RUN AWAY!
THERE IS CRABBY ROBOT-FACE! GET THEM!

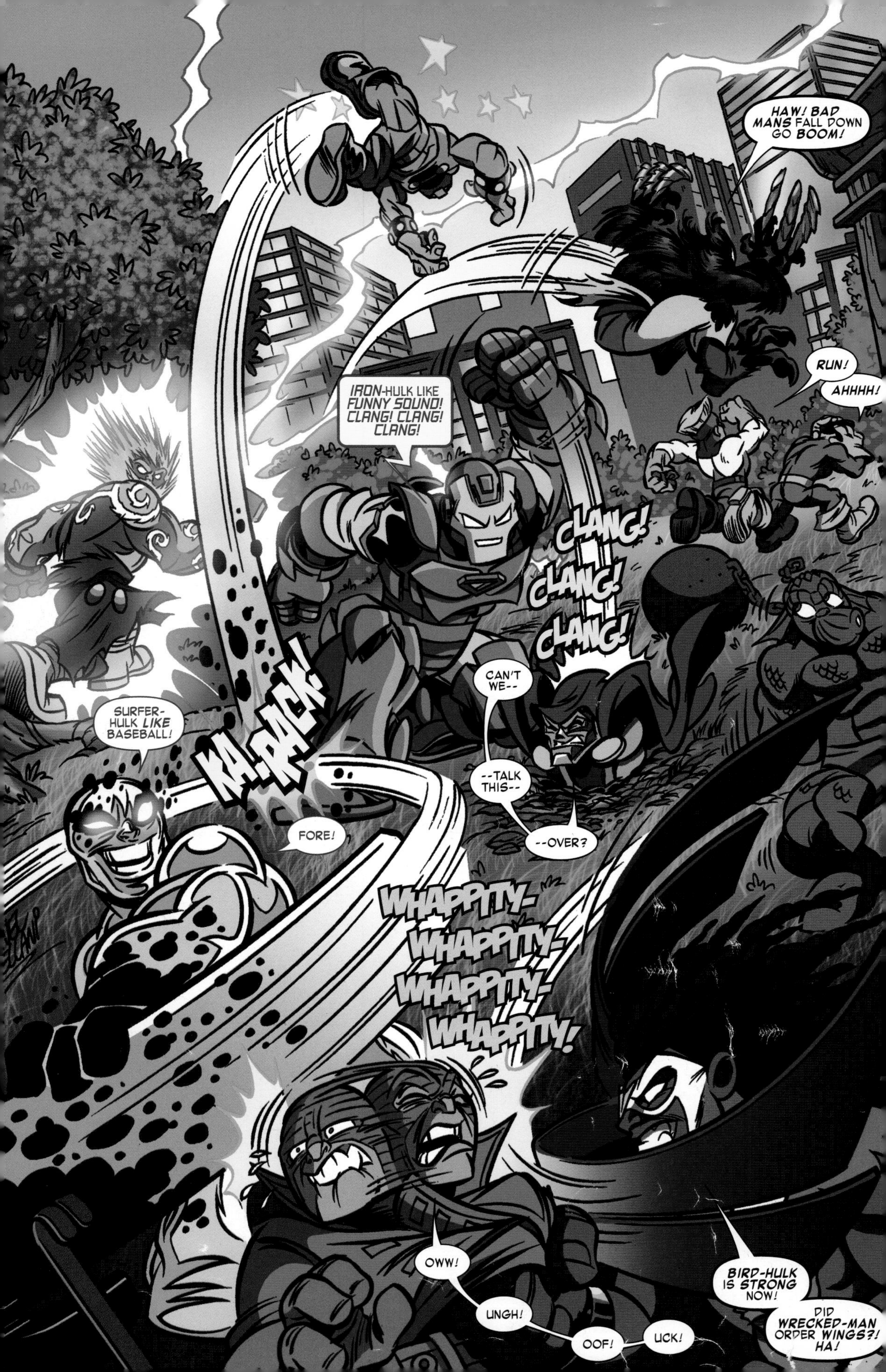
HAW! BAD MANS FALL DOWN GO BOOM!
RUN!
AHHHH!
IRON-HULK LIKE FUNNY SOUND! CLANG! CLANG! CLANG!
CLANG!
CLANG!
CLANG!
CAN'T WE--
--TALK THIS--
--OVER?
SURFER-HULK LIKE BASEBALL!
KA-RACK!
FORE!
WHAPPITTY-
WHAPPITTY-
WHAPPITTY-
WHAPPITTY!
OWW!
UNGH!
OOF!
UCK!
BIRD-HULK IS STRONG NOW!
DID WRECKED-MAN ORDER WINGS?! HA!

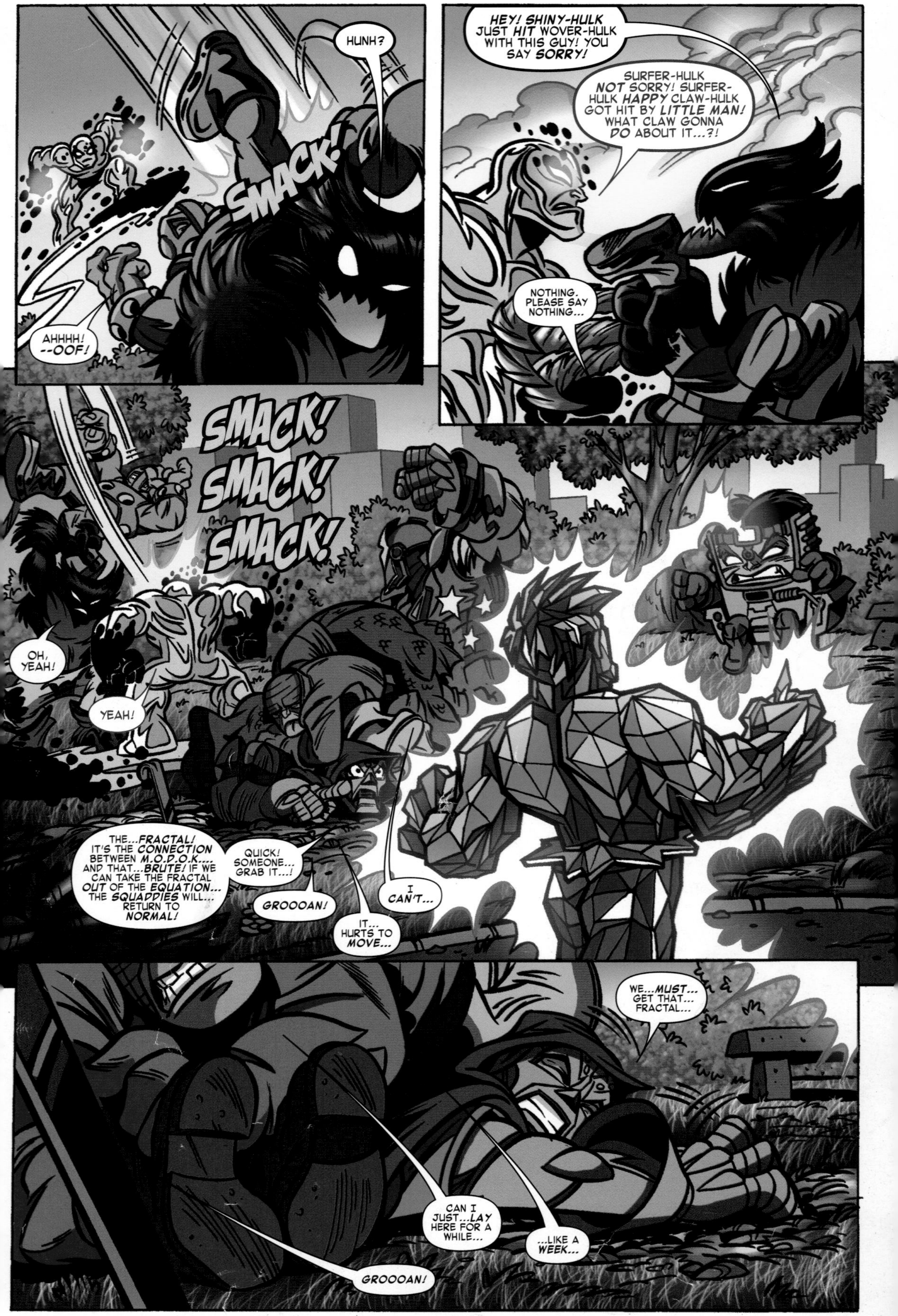
HUNH?
SMACK!
AHHHH! --OOF!
HEY! SHINY-HULK JUST HIT WOVER-HULK WITH THIS GUY! YOU SAY SORRY!
SURFER-HULK NOT SORRY! SURFER-HULK HAPPY CLAW-HULK GOT HIT BY LITTLE MAN! WHAT CLAW GONNA DO ABOUT IT...?!
NOTHING. PLEASE SAY NOTHING...
SMACK! SMACK! SMACK!
OH, YEAH!
YEAH!
THE...FRACTAL! IT'S THE CONNECTION BETWEEN M.O.D.O.K.... AND THAT...BRUTE! IF WE CAN TAKE THE FRACTAL OUT OF THE EQUATION... THE SQUADDIES WILL... RETURN TO NORMAL!
QUICK! SOMEONE... GRAB IT...!
GROOOAN!
I CAN'T...
IT... HURTS TO MOVE...
WE...MUST... GET THAT... FRACTAL...
CAN I JUST...LAY HERE FOR A WHILE...
...LIKE A WEEK...
GROOOAN!

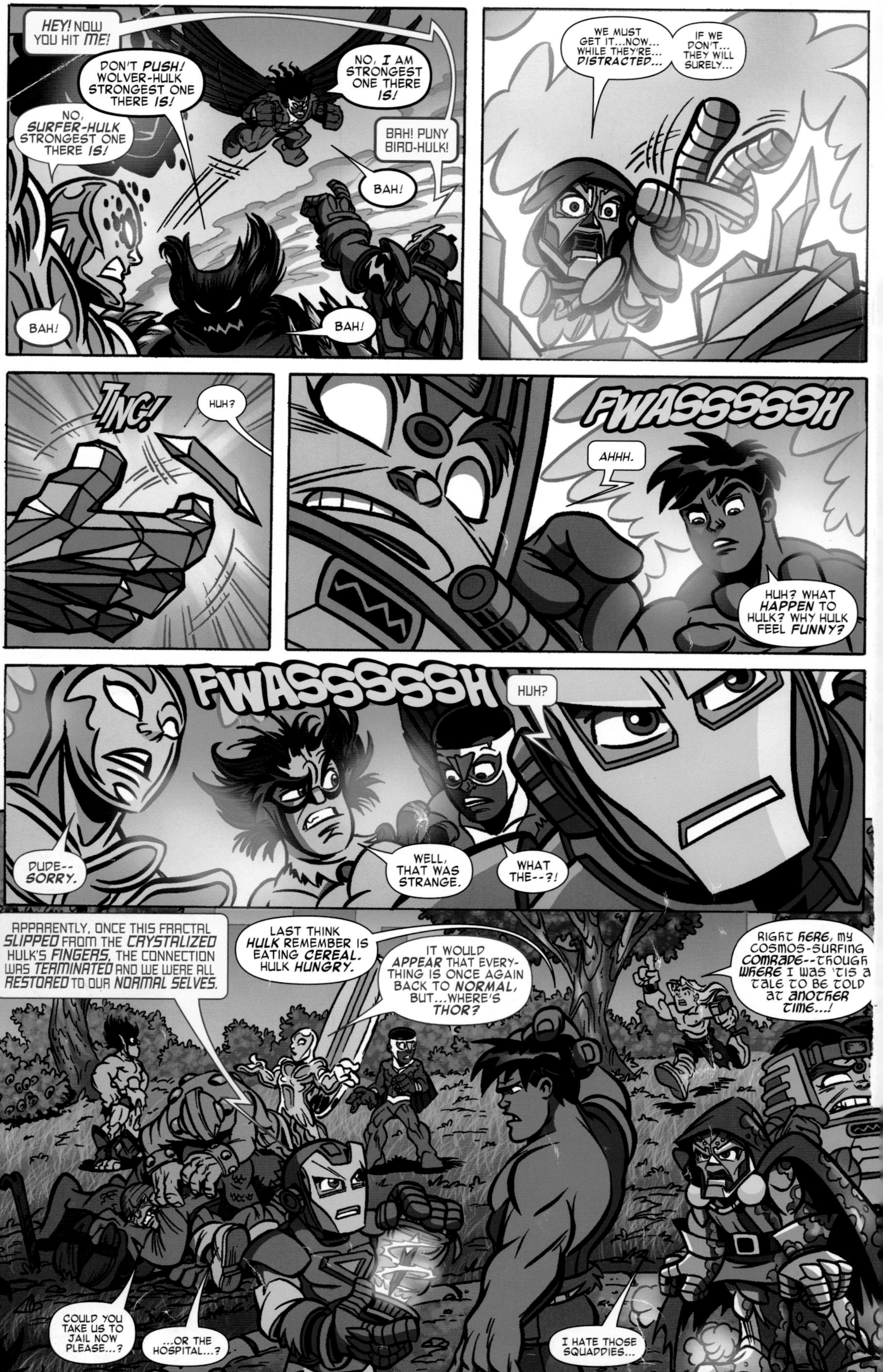
HEY! NOW YOU HIT ME!
DON'T PUSH! WOLVER-HULK STRONGEST ONE THERE IS!
NO, I AM STRONGEST ONE THERE IS!
NO, SURFER-HULK STRONGEST ONE THERE IS!
BAH! PUNY BIRD-HULK!
BAH!
BAH!
BAH!
WE MUST GET IT...NOW... WHILE THEY'RE... DISTRACTED...
IF WE DON'T... THEY WILL SURELY...
TING!
HUH?
FWASSSSSSH
AHHH.
HUH? WHAT HAPPEN TO HULK? WHY HULK FEEL FUNNY?
FWASSSSSSH
HUH?
DUDE-- SORRY.
WELL, THAT WAS STRANGE.
WHAT THE--?!
APPARENTLY, ONCE THIS FRACTAL SLIPPED FROM THE CRYSTALIZED HULK'S FINGERS, THE CONNECTION WAS TERMINATED AND WE WERE ALL RESTORED TO OUR NORMAL SELVES.
LAST THINK HULK REMEMBER IS EATING CEREAL. HULK HUNGRY.
IT WOULD APPEAR THAT EVERY-THING IS ONCE AGAIN BACK TO NORMAL, BUT...WHERE'S THOR?
RIGHT HERE, MY COSMOS-SURFING COMRADE--THOUGH WHERE I WAS 'TIS A TALE TO BE TOLD AT ANOTHER TIME...!
COULD YOU TAKE US TO JAIL NOW PLEASE...?
...OR THE HOSPITAL...?
I HATE THOSE SQUADDIES...

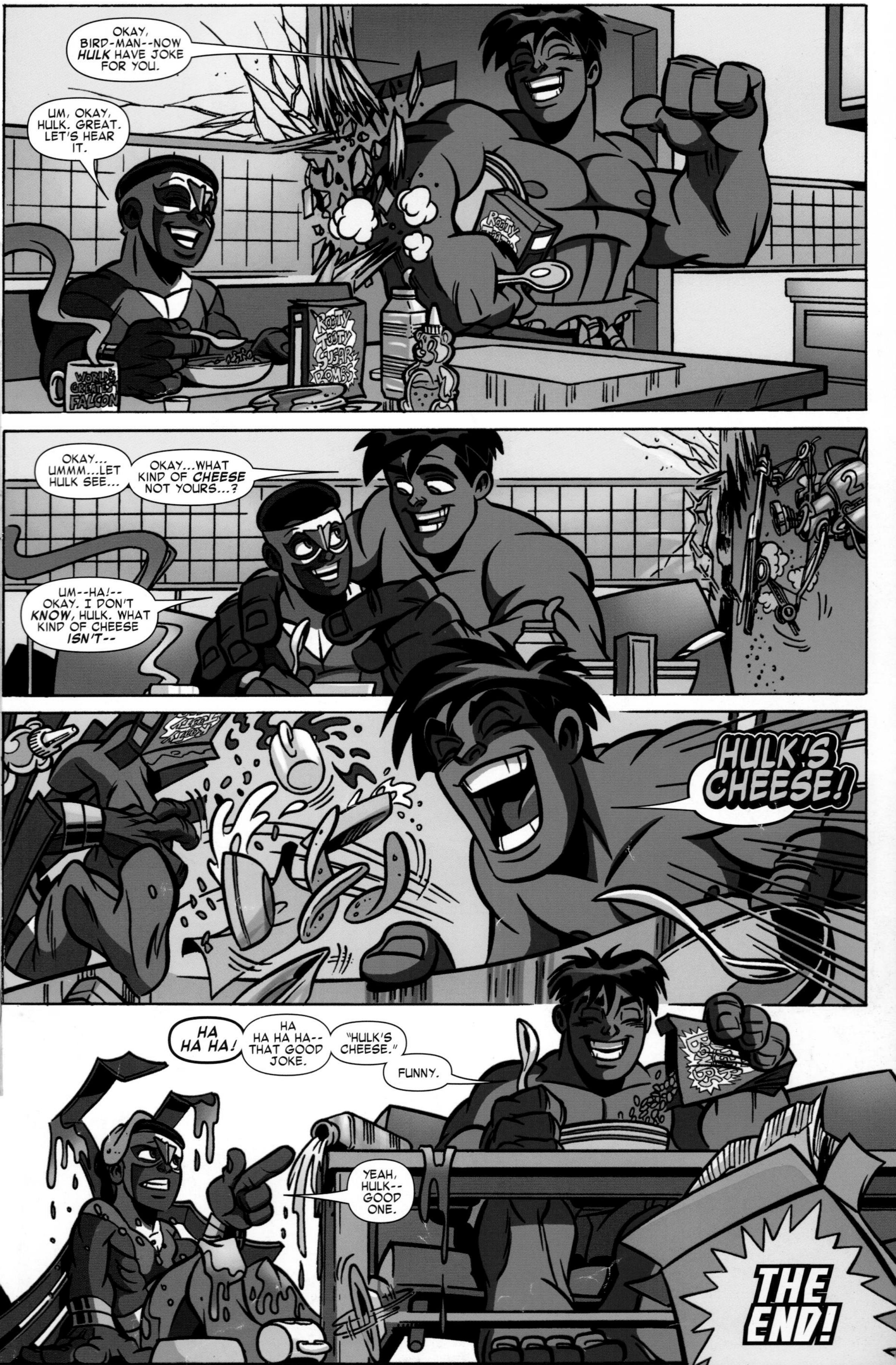
OKAY, BIRD-MAN--NOW HULK HAVE JOKE FOR YOU.
UM, OKAY, HULK. GREAT. LET'S HEAR IT.
WORLD'S GREATEST FALCON
ROOTY TOOTY SUGAR BOMBS
OKAY... UMMM...LET HULK SEE...
OKAY...WHAT KIND OF CHEESE NOT YOURS...?
UM--HA!--OKAY. I DON'T KNOW, HULK. WHAT KIND OF CHEESE ISN'T--
HULK'S CHEESE!
HA HA HA!
HA HA HA HA--THAT GOOD JOKE.
"HULK'S CHEESE."
FUNNY.
YEAH, HULK--GOOD ONE.
THE END!

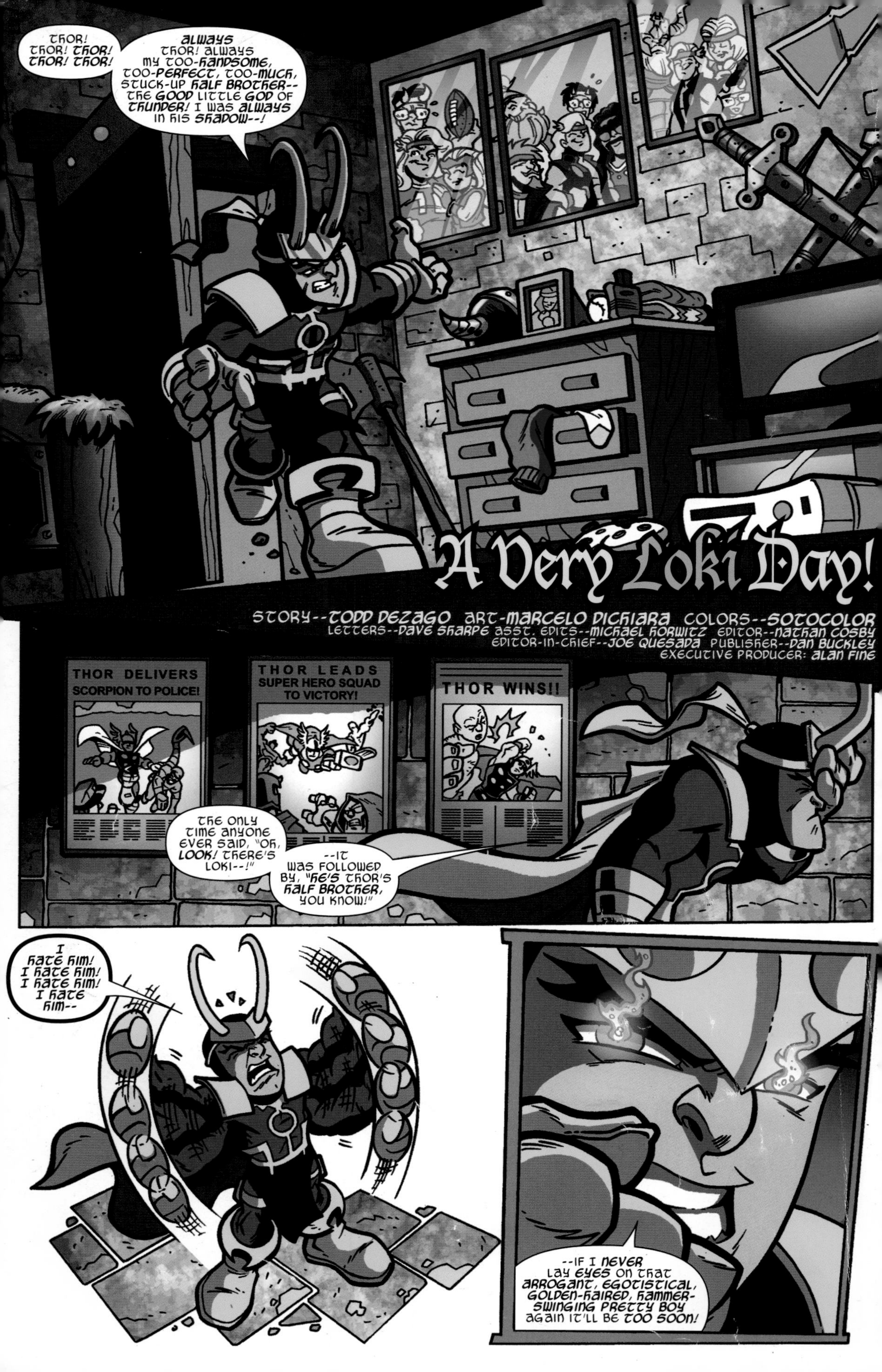
THOR! THOR! THOR! THOR! THOR!
ALWAYS THOR! ALWAYS MY TOO-HANDSOME, TOO-PERFECT, TOO-MUCH, STUCK-UP HALF BROTHER-- THE GOOD LITTLE GOD OF THUNDER! I WAS ALWAYS IN HIS SHADOW--!
A Very Loki Day!
STORY--TODD DEZAGO ART-MARCELO DICHIARA COLORS--SOTOCOLOR
LETTERS--DAVE SHARPE ASST. EDITS--MICHAEL HORWITZ EDITOR--NATHAN COSBY
EDITOR-IN-CHIEF--JOE QUESADA PUBLISHER--DAN BUCKLEY
EXECUTIVE PRODUCER: ALAN FINE
THOR DELIVERS SCORPION TO POLICE!
THOR LEADS SUPER HERO SQUAD TO VICTORY!
THOR WINS!!
THE ONLY TIME ANYONE EVER SAID, "OH, LOOK! THERE'S LOKI--!"
--IT WAS FOLLOWED BY, "HE'S THOR'S HALF BROTHER, YOU KNOW!"
I HATE HIM! I HATE HIM! I HATE HIM! I HATE HIM--
--IF I NEVER LAY EYES ON THAT ARROGANT, EGOTISTICAL, GOLDEN-HAIRED, HAMMER-SWINGING PRETTY BOY AGAIN IT'LL BE TOO SOON!

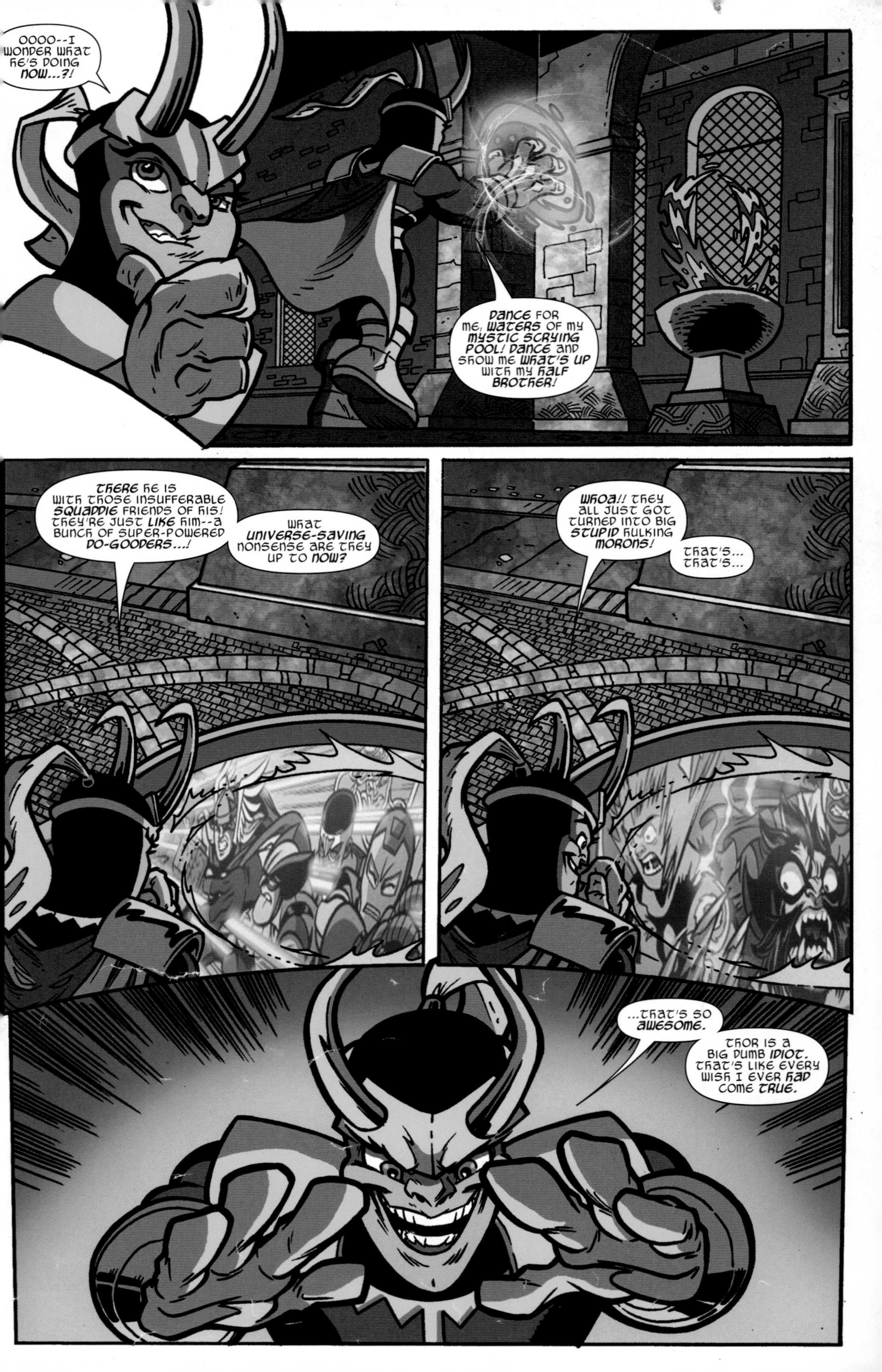

OOOO--I WONDER WHAT HE'S DOING NOW...?!
DANCE FOR ME, WATERS OF MY MYSTIC SCRYING POOL! DANCE AND SHOW ME WHAT'S UP WITH MY HALF BROTHER!
THERE HE IS WITH THOSE INSUFFERABLE SQUADDIE FRIENDS OF HIS! THEY'RE JUST LIKE HIM--A BUNCH OF SUPER-POWERED DO-GOODERS...!
WHAT UNIVERSE-SAVING NONSENSE ARE THEY UP TO NOW?
WHOA!! THEY ALL JUST GOT TURNED INTO BIG STUPID HULKING MORONS!
THAT'S... THAT'S...
...THAT'S SO AWESOME.
THOR IS A BIG DUMB IDIOT. THAT'S LIKE EVERY WISH I EVER HAD COME TRUE.

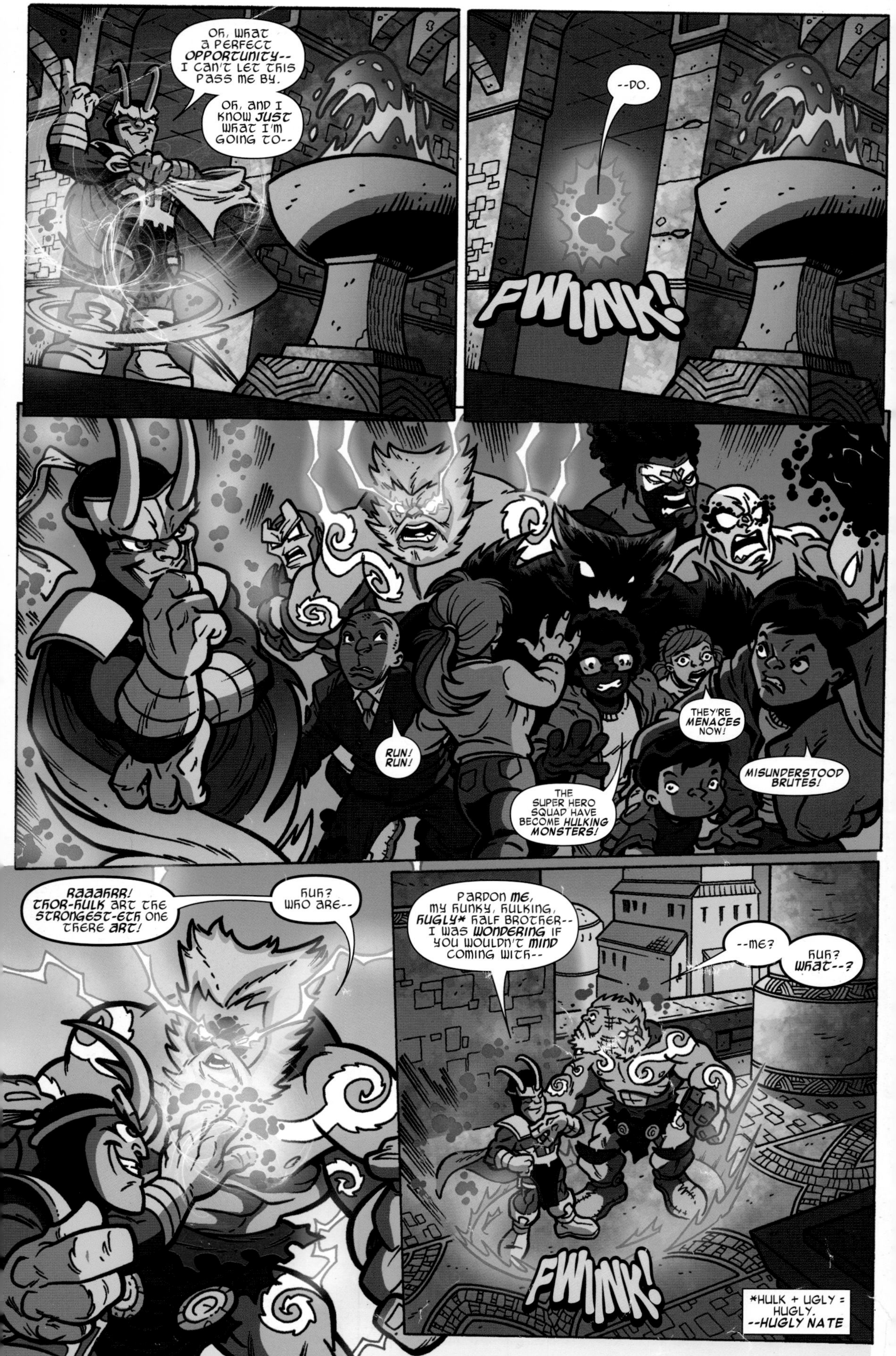

OH, WHAT A PERFECT OPPORTUNITY-- I CAN'T LET THIS PASS ME BY.
OH, AND I KNOW JUST WHAT I'M GOING TO--
--DO.
FWINK!
RUN! RUN!
THEY'RE MENACES NOW!
MISUNDERSTOOD BRUTES!
THE SUPER HERO SQUAD HAVE BECOME HULKING MONSTERS!
RAAAHRR! THOR-HULK ART THE STRONGEST-ETH ONE THERE ART!
HUH? WHO ARE--
PARDON ME, MY HUNKY, HULKING, HUGLY* HALF BROTHER-- I WAS WONDERING IF YOU WOULDN'T MIND COMING WITH--
--ME?
HUH? WHAT--?
FWINK!
*HULK + UGLY = HUGLY. --HUGLY NATE

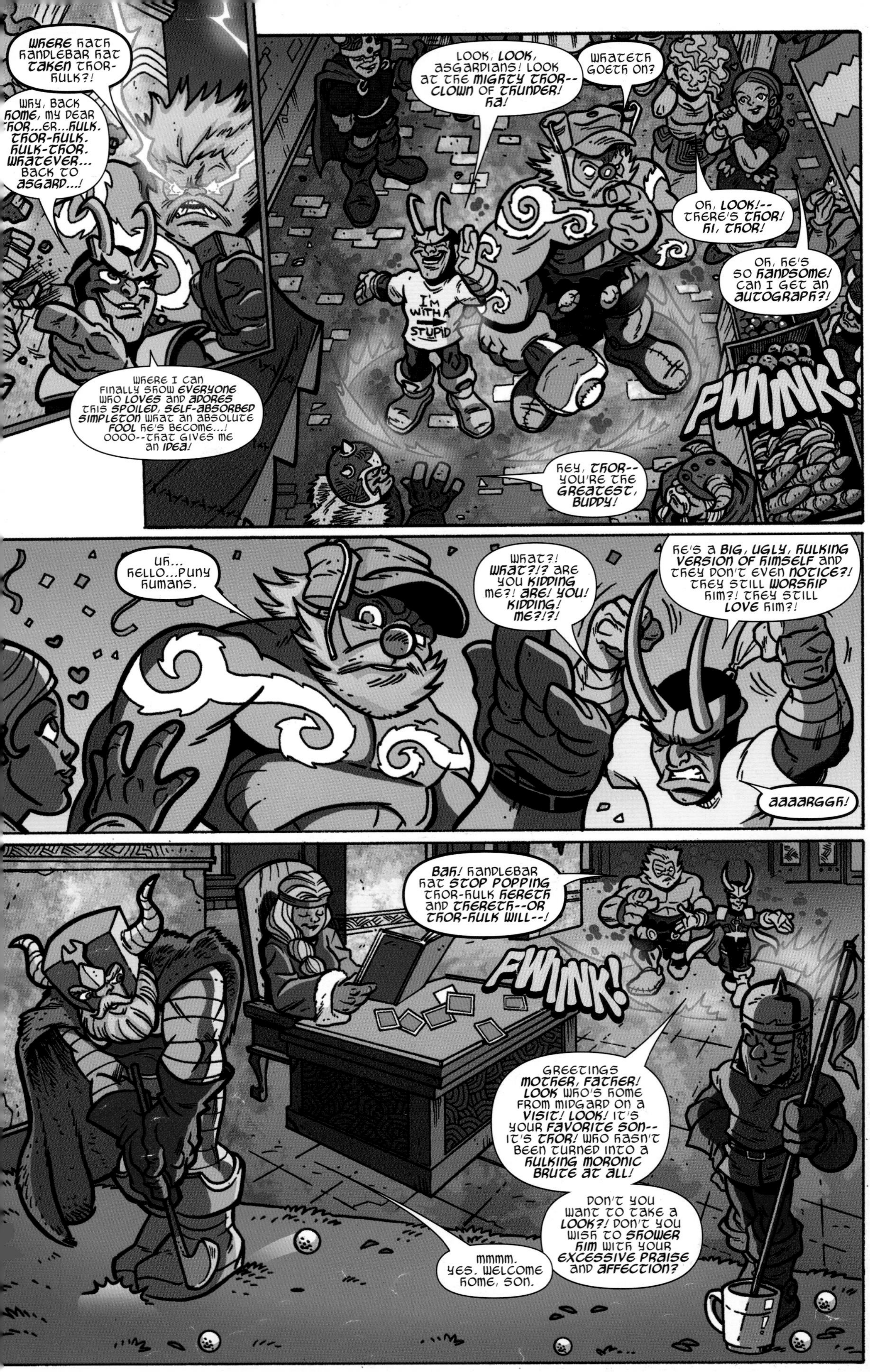
WHERE HATH HANDLEBAR HAT TAKEN THOR-HULK?!
WHY, BACK HOME, MY DEAR THOR...ER...HULK. THOR-HULK. HULK-THOR. WHATEVER... BACK TO ASGARD...!
WHERE I CAN FINALLY SHOW EVERYONE WHO LOVES AND ADORES THIS SPOILED, SELF-ABSORBED SIMPLETON WHAT AN ABSOLUTE FOOL HE'S BECOME...! OOOO--THAT GIVES ME AN IDEA!
LOOK, LOOK, ASGARDIANS! LOOK AT THE MIGHTY THOR--CLOWN OF THUNDER! HA!
I'M WITH A STUPID
WHATETH GOETH ON?
OH, LOOK!--THERE'S THOR! HI, THOR!
OH, HE'S SO HANDSOME! CAN I GET AN AUTOGRAPH?!
FWINK!
HEY, THOR--YOU'RE THE GREATEST, BUDDY!
UH... HELLO...PUNY HUMANS.
WHAT?! WHAT?!? ARE YOU KIDDING ME?! ARE! YOU! KIDDING! ME?!?!
HE'S A BIG, UGLY, HULKING VERSION OF HIMSELF AND THEY DON'T EVEN NOTICE?! THEY STILL WORSHIP HIM?! THEY STILL LOVE HIM?!
AAAARGGH!
BAH! HANDLEBAR HAT STOP POPPING THOR-HULK HERETH AND THERETH--OR THOR-HULK WILL--!
FWINK!
GREETINGS MOTHER, FATHER! LOOK WHO'S HOME FROM MIDGARD ON A VISIT! LOOK! IT'S YOUR FAVORITE SON--IT'S THOR! WHO HASN'T BEEN TURNED INTO A HULKING MORONIC BRUTE AT ALL!
DON'T YOU WANT TO TAKE A LOOK?! DON'T YOU WISH TO SHOWER HIM WITH YOUR EXCESSIVE PRAISE AND AFFECTION?
MMMM. YES. WELCOME HOME, SON.

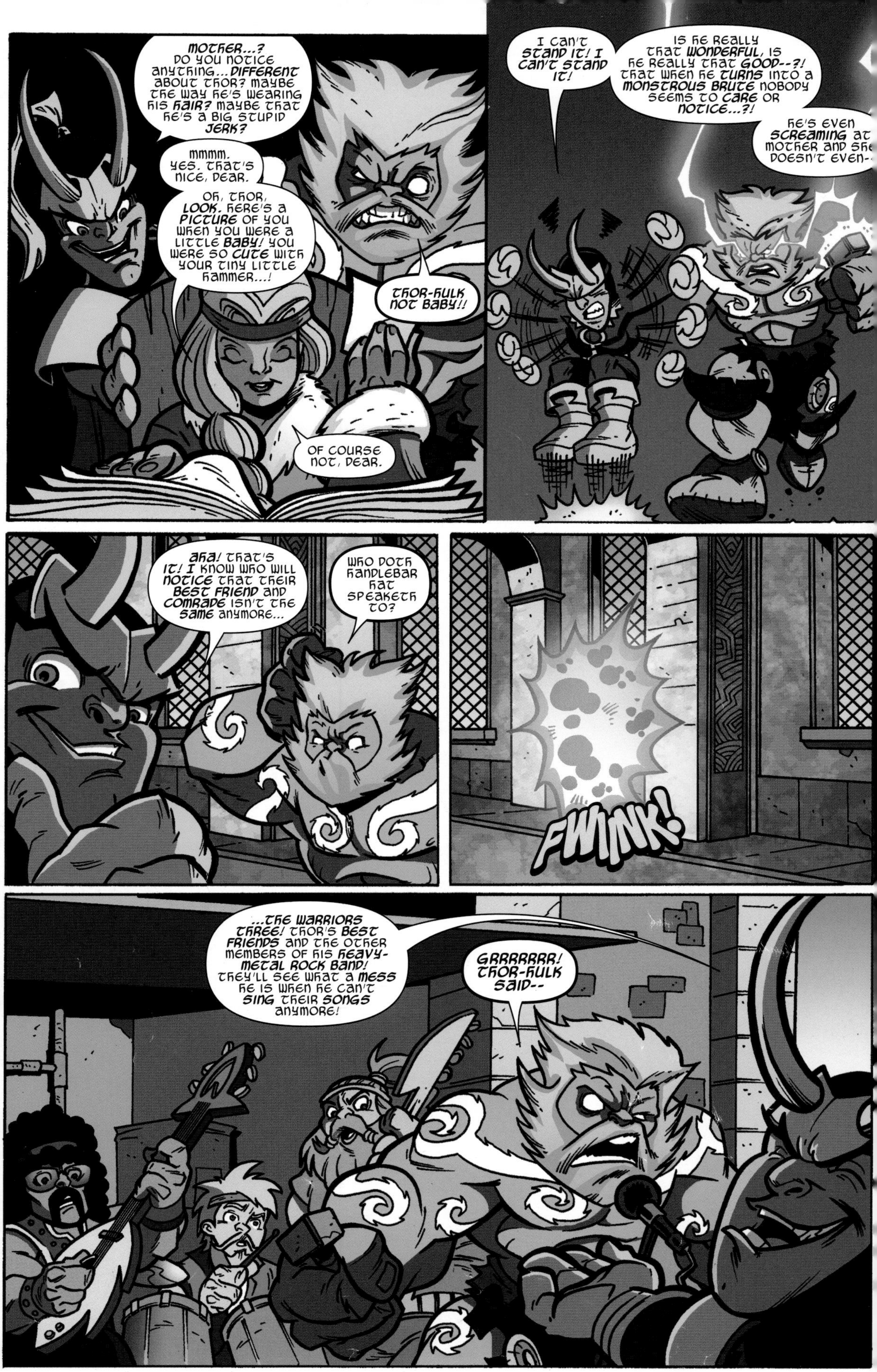
MOTHER...? DO YOU NOTICE ANYTHING... DIFFERENT ABOUT THOR? MAYBE THE WAY HE'S WEARING HIS HAIR? MAYBE THAT HE'S A BIG STUPID JERK?
MMMM. YES. THAT'S NICE, DEAR.
OH, THOR, LOOK. HERE'S A PICTURE OF YOU WHEN YOU WERE A LITTLE BABY! YOU WERE SO CUTE WITH YOUR TINY LITTLE HAMMER...!
THOR-HULK NOT BABY!!
OF COURSE NOT, DEAR.
I CAN'T STAND IT! I CAN'T STAND IT!
IS HE REALLY THAT WONDERFUL, IS HE REALLY THAT GOOD--?! THAT WHEN HE TURNS INTO A MONSTROUS BRUTE NOBODY SEEMS TO CARE OR NOTICE...?!
HE'S EVEN SCREAMING AT MOTHER AND SHE DOESN'T EVEN--
AHA! THAT'S IT! I KNOW WHO WILL NOTICE THAT THEIR BEST FRIEND AND COMRADE ISN'T THE SAME ANYMORE...
WHO DOTH HANDLEBAR HAT SPEAKETH TO?
FWINK!
...THE WARRIORS THREE! THOR'S BEST FRIENDS AND THE OTHER MEMBERS OF HIS HEAVY-METAL ROCK BAND! THEY'LL SEE WHAT A MESS HE IS WHEN HE CAN'T SING THEIR SONGS ANYMORE!
GRRRRRRR! THOR-HULK SAID--

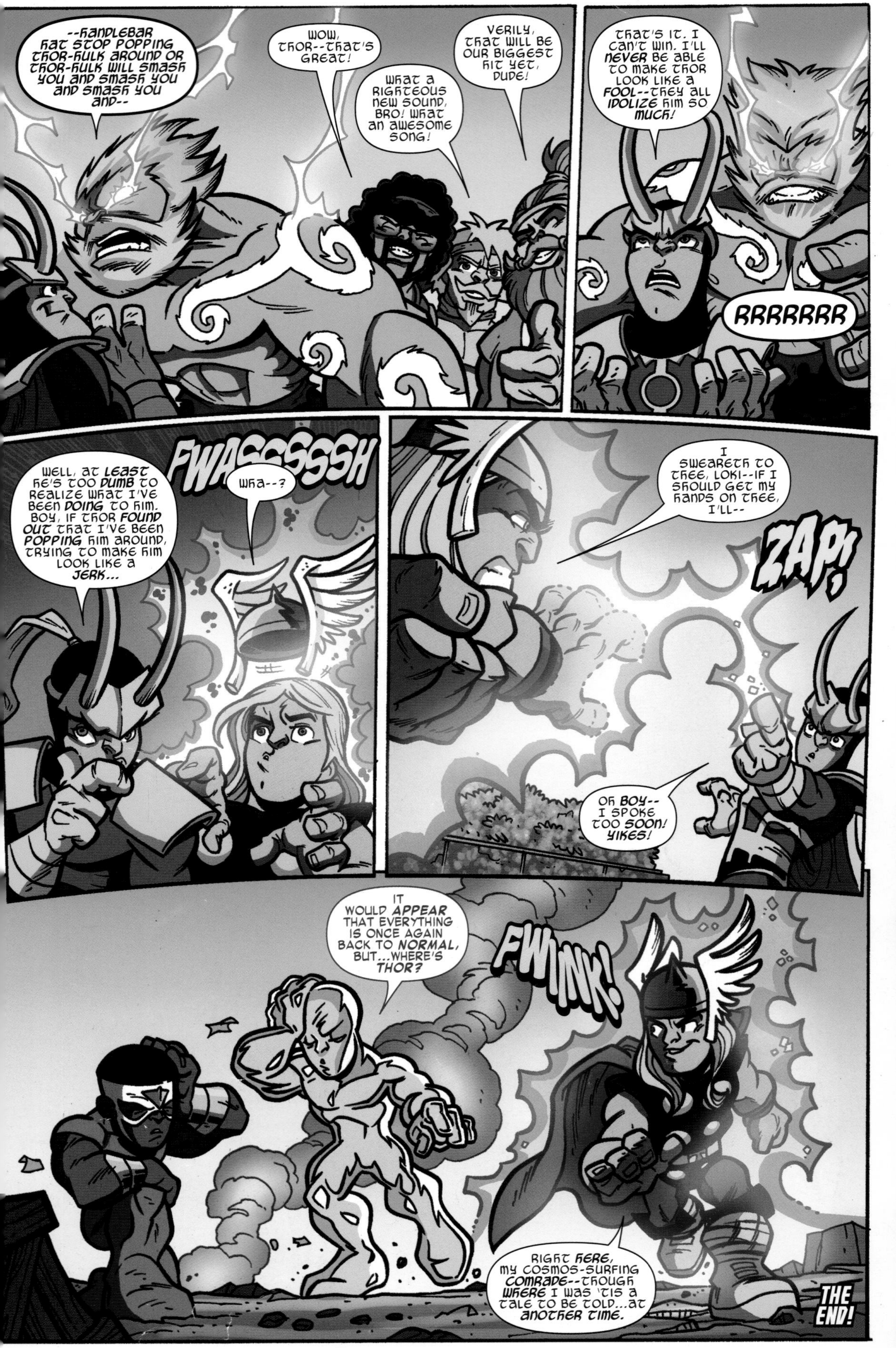
--HANDLEBAR HAT STOP POPPING THOR-HULK AROUND OR THOR-HULK WILL SMASH YOU AND SMASH YOU AND SMASH YOU AND--
WOW, THOR--THAT'S GREAT!
WHAT A RIGHTEOUS NEW SOUND, BRO! WHAT AN AWESOME SONG!
VERILY, THAT WILL BE OUR BIGGEST HIT YET, DUDE!
THAT'S IT. I CAN'T WIN. I'LL NEVER BE ABLE TO MAKE THOR LOOK LIKE A FOOL--THEY ALL IDOLIZE HIM SO MUCH!
RRRRRRR
WELL, AT LEAST HE'S TOO DUMB TO REALIZE WHAT I'VE BEEN DOING TO HIM. BOY, IF THOR FOUND OUT THAT I'VE BEEN POPPING HIM AROUND, TRYING TO MAKE HIM LOOK LIKE A JERK...
FWASSSSSH
WHA--?
I SWEARETH TO THEE, LOKI--IF I SHOULD GET MY HANDS ON THEE, I'LL--
ZAP!
OH BOY-- I SPOKE TOO SOON! YIKES!
IT WOULD APPEAR THAT EVERYTHING IS ONCE AGAIN BACK TO NORMAL, BUT...WHERE'S THOR?
FWINK!
RIGHT HERE, MY COSMOS-SURFING COMRADE--THOUGH WHERE I WAS 'TIS A TALE TO BE TOLD...AT ANOTHER TIME.
THE END!

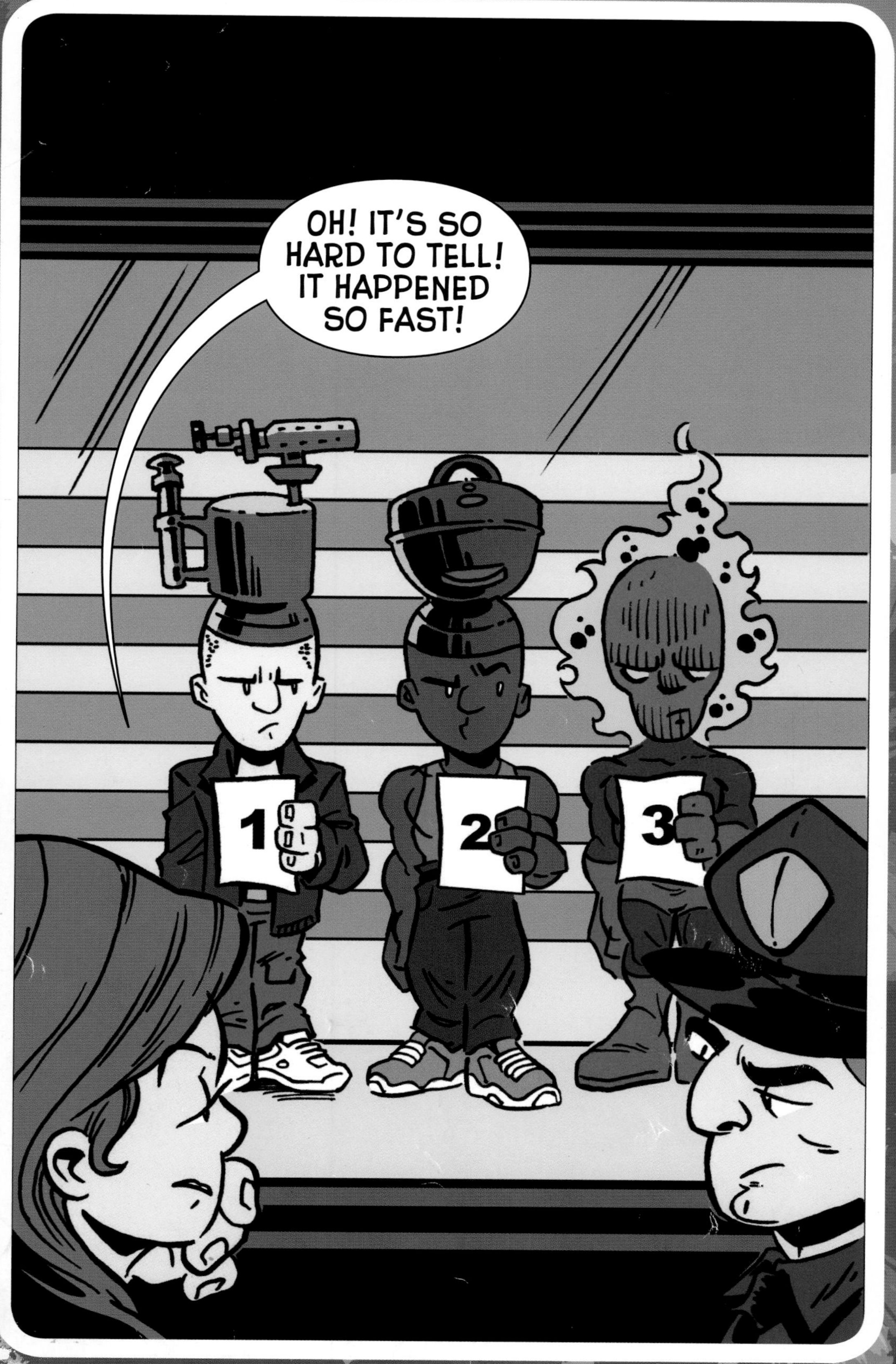
OH! IT'S SO HARD TO TELL! IT HAPPENED SO FAST!
1
2
3

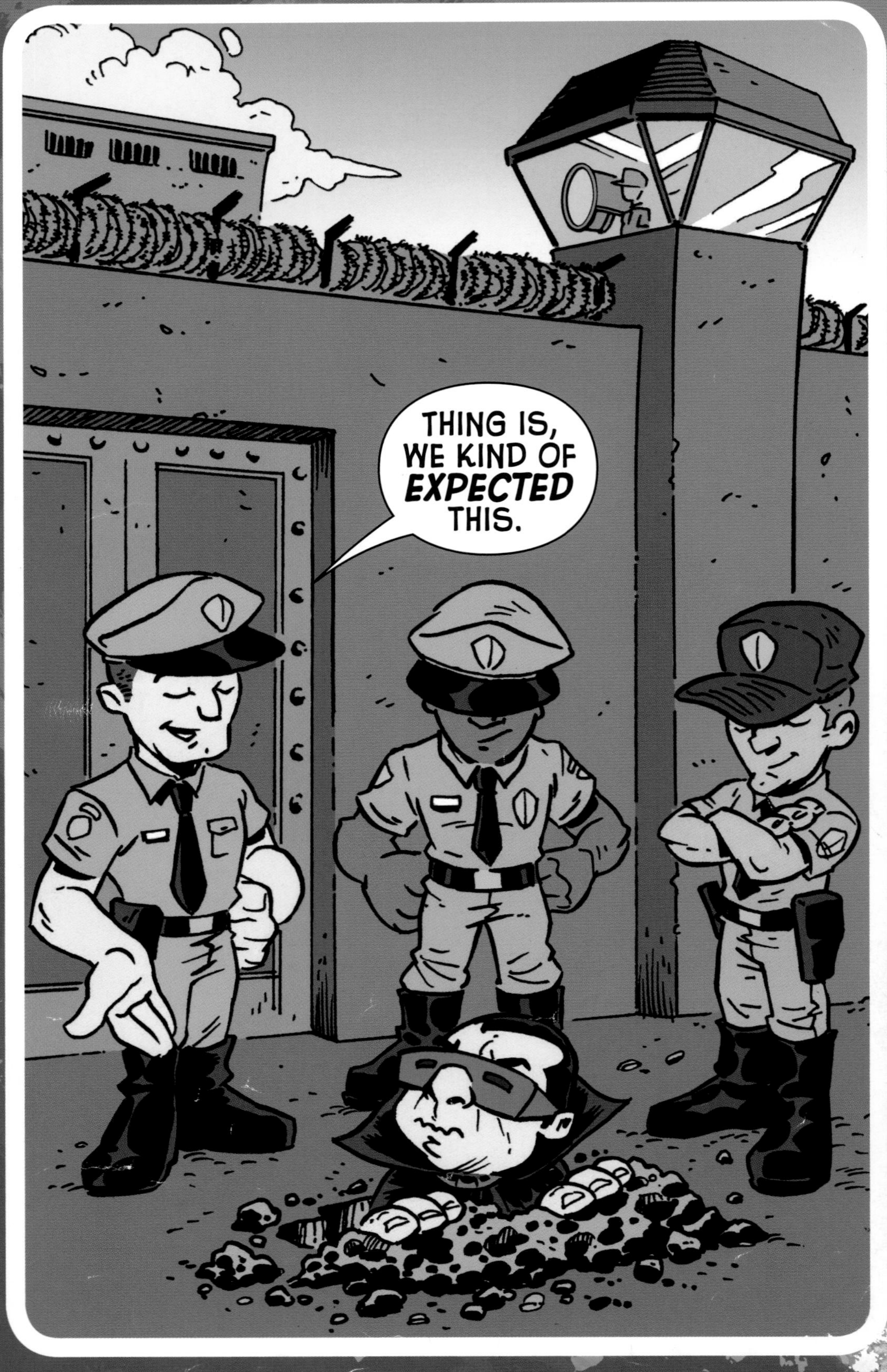
THING IS, WE KIND OF *EXPECTED* THIS.

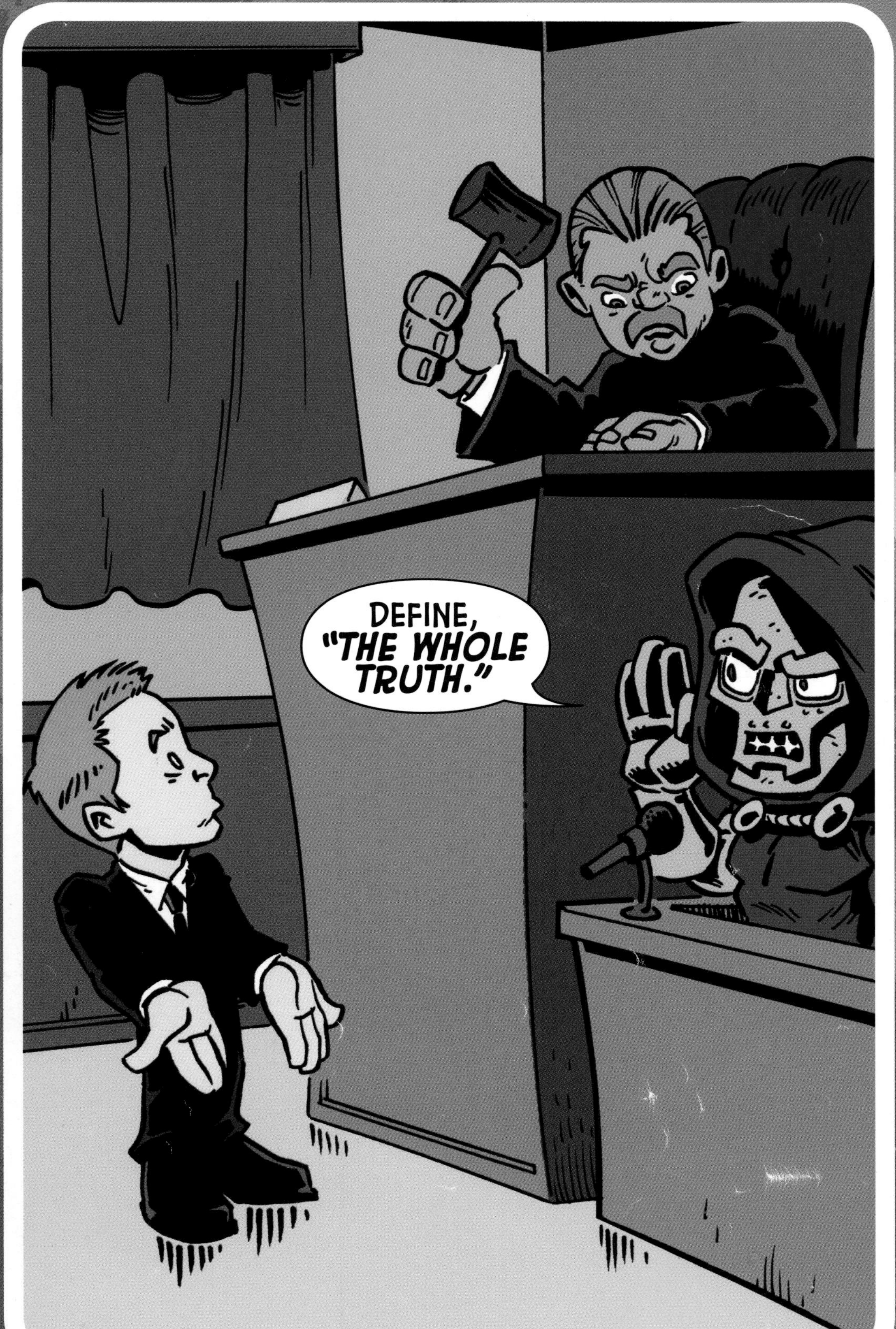
DEFINE, "THE WHOLE TRUTH."

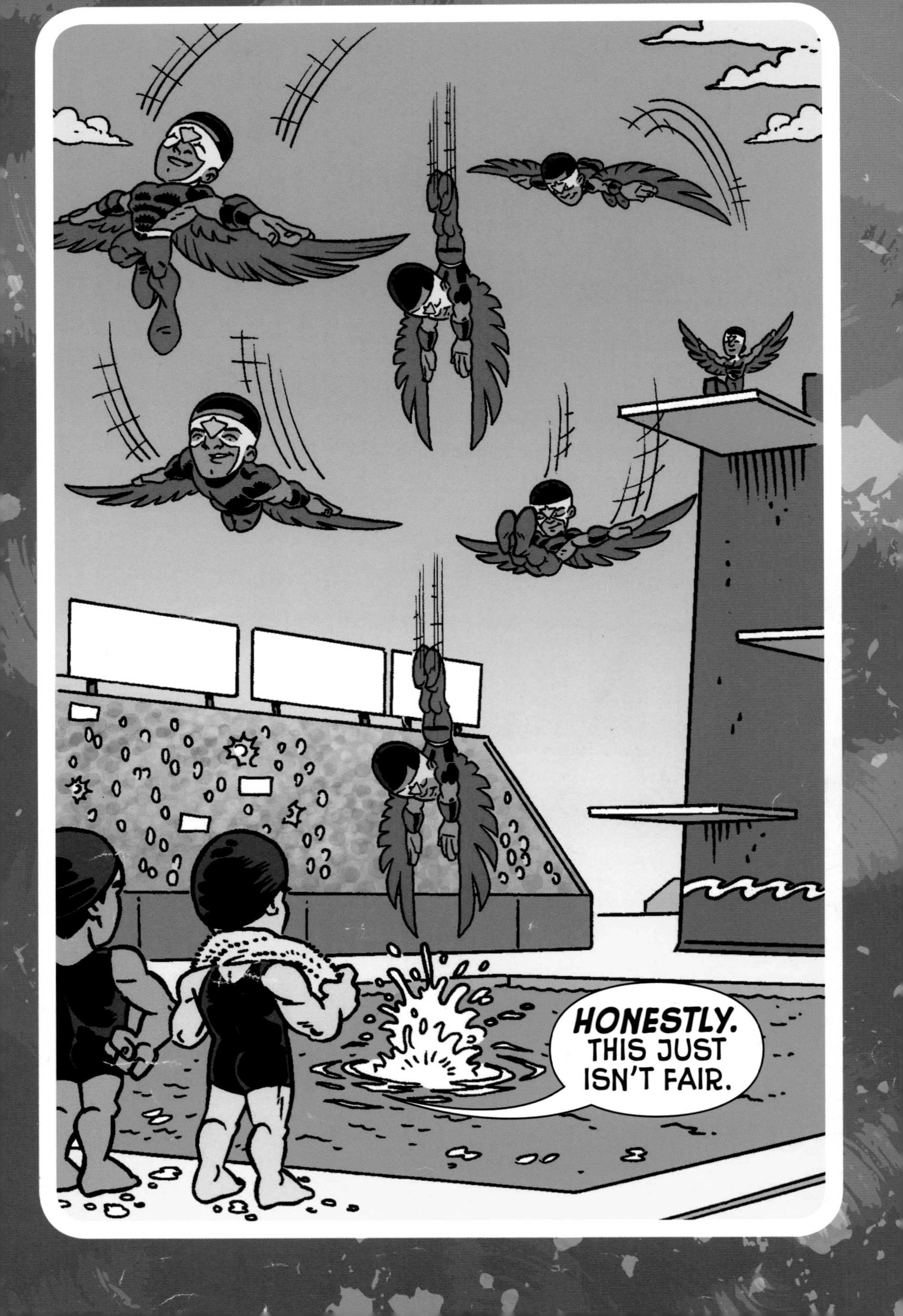
HONESTLY. THIS JUST ISN'T FAIR.

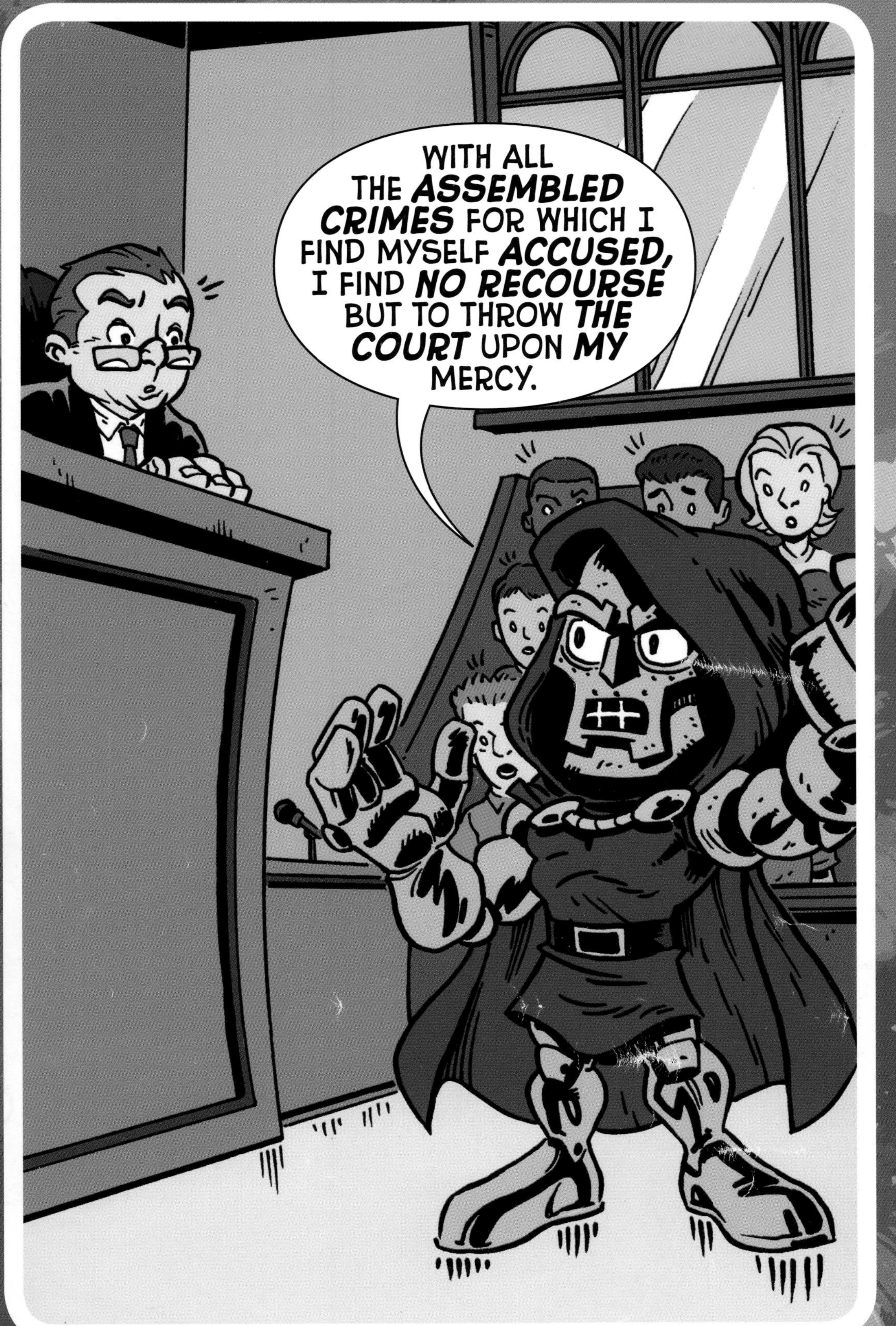
WITH ALL THE ASSEMBLED CRIMES FOR WHICH I FIND MYSELF ACCUSED, I FIND NO RECOURSE BUT TO THROW THE COURT UPON MY MERCY.